A Layman's Understanding of Satan's Evil!

A Layman's Understanding of Satan's Evil!

ALAN SHINKFIELD

Copyright © 2021 Alan Shinkfield.

All rights reserved. No part of this book may be reproduced in any form or by any electronic or mechanical means, including information storage and retrieval systems, without permission in writing from the publisher, except by reviewers, who may quote brief passages in a review.

ISBN: 978-1-63821-026-9 (Paperback Edition)
ISBN: 978-1-63821-027-6 (Hardcover Edition)
ISBN: 978-1-63821-025-2 (E-book Edition)

Scripture taken from Holy Bible, New International Version®, NIV® Copyright ©1973, 1978, 1984, 2011 by Biblica, Inc.® Used by permission. All rights reserved worldwide.

Book Ordering Information

Phone Number: 315 288-7939 ext. 1000 or 347-901-4920
Email: info@globalsummithouse.com
Global Summit House
www.globalsummithouse.com

Printed in the United State of America

The Destruction Caused by Satan's Evil!

Because evil is destructive, it will become a danger to its-self by reason of its ever growing desire to see everything in ruins, it will eventually destroy all, no matter if it be good or evil. Somehow in my mind this proves what a strict disciplinarian Satan is, he keeps his troops in complete order. His followers, demons, false prophets, betrayers of God's laws, in fact any person that has not accepted the word of God and his Son Jesus Christ as their Saviour, is truly confined to a life dedicated to evil by the head evil one himself.

Christians on the other hand are very busy following the doctrine of their preferred denomination rather than the true and spiritual Christianity as handed down by our leader. We fear being called names; we fear opinions of friends and relations who have never experienced the movement of the Holy Spirit in their lives. We fear becoming outcasts in the social circles about us; we fear the scorn of family and work-mates as we endeavour to live a life full of love and compassion.

I want you to answer honestly to God, as you are given a free will by the Father of all living things, why don't you follow him instead of the evil one who requires nothing of you but your useless and defeated soul? Christianity was made for today and today for you is decision time. Look on your calendar is tomorrow listed? We do know

Jesus Christ will return and by the logic of no tomorrows, he will return today!

Today, when you wake this morning may be the last day of living your life, as you now know it. Are you prepared? Whilst answering questions, try this one, but again be as honest with yourself as if standing before a judge who knows all. Today you receive the news from your doctor or hospital that you have twenty-four hours to live, would you spend those hours in cursing and blaming God for the terrible hand fate has dealt you?

Would you be perfectly honest and blame the cigarettes, alcohol, drugs, and your lack of healthy living? Or would you rely on the promises of Jesus and claim through his sacrificial blood complete forgiveness and seek his mercy to save you?

It is too late to take out an insurance policy when your house has burnt down or your car wrecked, or a funeral-plan the day after you had died. With these things in mind and when you come to judgement before the Highest Power to receive your sentence in Hades or reward in Heaven, do not call on God with the excuse you were going to do it tomorrow, he may just point to the calendar and ask you, "Where is tomorrow?" Try and live with this every day, you don't know when will be the time or date of your expiry from earth?

A car accident on the way to work, dumped by a wave while enjoying the beach, a fatal disease, the only certainty in life is death. According to God's word your choice to be made while living in this world, is, do you want eternity in Heaven with the good God or eternity in hell with the prince of darkness? The one who has proven his love for you, or the one who wants a completely destroyed shattered life, it's your decision to make now.

The sincere message from this book, if you or I should die tomorrow, (which is today yesterday), or Jesus could return on that day, what provision have you made for the afterlife? Are you as certain there is nothing after death as I am that there is? For if you are not, then you will have big trouble explaining why you believe what you do before the Judgement Throne.

Has your judgement been created because you have listened and accepted, without study, what you have been told? Have you ever bothered to obtain for yourself a book upon the subject in question, and perused it and compared that to your God given common sense?

Although there are only ten commandments they cover many other laws, they can be broadened to cover all the laws handed down to the Jewish Nation as set out in Leviticus. As there is one commandment on adultery, there are eighteen variations listed of sexual relationships that are forbidden by God. None one has been rescinded by Jesus' teachings, as he taught throughout his earthly ministry, Paul in most of his letters condemns what we seem to accept today.

The breaking of these laws have the prescribed sentence, death. This of course was the end of earthly life, there are some that will believe these sentences were extreme. We are fortunate Jesus was crucified as a sacrifice for our sins, now the sentence is the loss of eternal life, which is far lot longer than the life we experience here. Do not be mislead, you must accept and acknowledge, that if you do not have eternal life in heaven you will spend it in Hades and in torment.

So it follows there has only been one who lived in perfect communion and followed the laws and commandments and He was the Son of God, the promised Messiah, Jesus Christ, who became the true and only sacrifice without blemish. How difficult is it for man to believe such a simple and effective plan, we as true Christians cannot understand why men's minds are so clouded by earthly treasures that they ignore the truth.

Luke, chapter 15 verses 4 & 5. *"Suppose one of you has a hundred sheep and looses one of them. Does he not leave the ninety-nine in the open country and go after the lost sheep until he finds it? And when he finds it, he joyfully puts it on his shoulders and goes home."*

As Jesus did, we as Christians must weep, search and find the lamb that went astray from all those already in the fold. We must question why this is happening when we have access to that great power that covers all the resources and wisdom of God, to lead us into the ultimate victory against Satan when we shall welcome the second coming of the true Messiah only this time recognising Him as the Son of God and our only Saviour and mediator.

This book is not meant to make you feel comfortable, nor complacent, for when we compare our lives with the life of Jesus, we have never suffered as He did. I would like to share with you some wisdom that I received some time ago. I do not know who wrote it, a it was inspired by a greater wisdom than mine. As we read it, seek out the truth, he was contented with what he had and where he travelled and with whom he spoke, he forgave all who transpired to end his earthly commitments.

JESUS DIED FOR OUR SINS!

The greatest man in history,
Jesus had no servants,
yet they called him Master.
Had no degree, yet they called him teacher.
Had no medicines, yet they called him healer.
Had no army, yet kings feared him.
He won no military battles,
yet he conquered the world.
He committed no crime,
yet they crucified him.
They buried him in a tomb, yet he lives today.
I am honoured to serve such a leader,
and you can join me.
If you love and believe in God,
and his Son Jesus Christ.
If you don't believe,
don't ignore this message,
Just remember Jesus warned,
"If you deny me before man,
I will deny you before my Father in Heaven."
And he will finish what he started.

Exodus chapter 20 and verse 7, the second commandment, ***"You shall not misuse the name of the Lord your God, for the Lord will not hold anyone guiltless who misuses his name."*** Yet every day in real life, on our television screens, on radio, people of every walk of life, exclaim when something good, bad, or surprising, "oh my God" This would not be quite so bad if it was "oh my god". To all these unthinking people, accept that you will not be held blameless when you stand before the Judgement Throne, and be sure that you will be called to judgement.

In Leviticus 19: 28, ***"Do not cut your bodies for the dead or put tattoo marks on yourselves. I am the Lord."*** Adolph Hitler knew much about the Jewish faith and the laws in Leviticus, and to demean the Jews further he ordered every one of them was to have a number as a tattoo on their arm, against the very laws handed down by God. In verse 31 ***"Do not turn to mediums or seek out spiritualists, you will be defiled by them. I am the Lord your God."*** How many of us look to those who claim to have the power to tell the future? You have broken a law from God.

At 83 years of age, of course I like verse 32, ***"Rise in the presence of the aged, show respect for the elderly and revere your God. I am the Lord."*** Most of us who are in the elderly age group were always taught these things, respect your elders and it did apply to all. In this evil world where Satan reigns, we read daily of elderly being attacked robbed, scammed by younger people who have the fitness but not the will to work for financial reward.

It was protocol, it was manners, all families taught them. Unfortunately over two generations, the community by and large does not know or care that God is Lord, they are never taught respect, they are never shown discipline, and therefore all the community suffers as they believe in their own importance and that the world owes them a living.

What about Sunday or the Sabbath as described in God's laws, chapter 23 of Leviticus verse 3, ***"There are six days when you may work, but the seventh day is a Sabbath of rest, a day of sacred assembly. You are not to do any work; wherever you live, it is a Sabbath to the Lord."***

There are those who will quote Jesus, who defended the disciples from picking corn and eating grain on the Sabbath. Matthew's Gospel chapter 12, covers Jesus as Lord of the Sabbath and in verse 11, *"He said to them, 'If any of you has a sheep and it falls into a pit on the Sabbath; will you not take hold of it and lift it out? How much more valuable is a man than a sheep! Therefore it is lawful to do good on the Sabbath."*

What is the good that can be done on the Sabbath? Doctors, hospitals, emergency workers, the police, consider if you will Sunday without a policeman on duty, the Clergy of course, missions that support the destitute, parents. Those who contribute in some way to the less fortunate, the emergency workers many of whom are volunteers and are subject to loss, as those who they help.

The world has changed, sport now encroaches upon the Sabbath, as does the trading for profit, we can rather go to many entertainments rather than worship.

What then is not so good that is done on the Sabbath and therefore breaks the laws of God? As Leviticus warns, "but the seventh day is a day of rest, *a day of sacred assembly.*" So I would say topping the list at number one is, not attending an organised worship centre or church in a family group or individually.

Closely following would be supporting any organised event, sporting or entertainment that is being used for financial gain. Just think of the power shown by the Christian community if all Christians did boycott sporting fixtures. Specially holding their children away from junior fixtures on a Sabbath or Sunday.

Try going to the movies on any day but Sunday or your Sabbath, don't buy a Sunday newspaper, on Sundays don't watch television, don't listen to the radio, this would become not profitable and the promoters would soon cancel such events.

Hands up all those who said **"HOW BORING."** What will we do? You will do what we did in the times when the Sabbath was respected; we spent time with our families, not only our children but also all our relations, cousins, grandparents aunts and uncles. Friends are very important to our earthly life cycle. They lift us when we are down and share our troubles.

We learnt how good it was to be accepted as part of a wider group of people. Family outings, car trips to see and appreciate God's great handiwork, now of course much of this beauty is covered by man's desire for bigger accommodation, for spas and swimming pools.

A trip to the beach was a great day of bonding, and not expensive, although we did depend on those who were responsible for the safety on the beach, the life-savers, who also performed good deeds on the Sabbath. It always astonishes one when one considers the beauty of a tree and when man has fashioned it for his use as an electricity pole it becomes a lifeless stick without any semblance of the beauty it once represented.

Is this another victory for man's ingenuity? We are able to tear down all that is beautiful and replace it with half-baked notions that we can do it better than the original Creator. Look how we treat God's great love and the sacrifice Jesus Christ made. We desecrate the Lord's Sabbath, by attending sporting fixtures. Of course we take our family with us for time together and then show our children how to swear at umpires and referees.

We boo the opposition when they make a great play and score, and generally teach those with us how to behave in an non-sportsman like manner. When we get home and our children use the words that we have just used in front of them, we chastise them for not obeying our wishes, yet not long before hand we applauded sportsmen or women for not obeying the laws as laid down by the head official.

Have you ever watched a football match on television, and seen the expressions of complete hatred which cover supporters faces when a decision is made against their team, at that time murder is not far beneath their feelings.

It is easy now to see why Jesus extended the commandments to include the thoughts of thing denied.

This is why Jesus warned us in Matthew 5, chapter verses 21 to 23, ***"You have heard that it was said to the people, 'Do not murder and anyone who murders will be subject to judgement.' But I tell you that anyone who is angry with his brother will be subject to judgement."***

Although Jesus spoke about gouging your eye out or cutting off you arm if they caused you to sin; you should definitely stay away from sporting or other fixtures if you are emotionally affected by what you see. Do not place yourself in positions where your hot-blooded feelings could cause danger to those around you.

Emotions must be controlled if we are going to live in a world of peace and harmony; do we have to take everything on a serious note? Do we have to have revenge for every thing that is done against us or our loved ones?

We are now at a stage when the most trivial altercation flares into a fight causing serious injury or death. Is it worth it? Lives are ruined and Satan laughs! We have to learn that complete control over all our emotions is a must for the peace of God to spread throughout the entire world.

Even the emotion of love, once revered as a Holy ordinance, can quickly change into lust and damage two people who should have respect and cherish each others moral standards. There is no doubt that unless we can keep our emotions in control, we shall destroy a peaceful and joyous time on earth and relinquish all opportunities of dwelling with God in Heaven.

Is it worth a moment of temper to gain instant revenge? We can blame alcohol, drugs, our childhood, our parent's failure, and even some wish to lay the blame on my

God. Who but you drank the alcohol? You administered the drugs, were our parents beside us when we committed the offence. Excuses are fine, and are recognised in many courts, but consider this, God knows all, and His judgement will be based on truth.

Your actions will be judged as your actions, and you will be held accountable in the great courtroom, and the Judge will be the only one who lived a life without ever loosing control of His emotions. Every person has emotions; it is how they control these emotions which prove the moral and ethical standards by which we live.

Questions never asked and therefore never answered concern the behaviour of children, young adults and even into their later years, by their parents, who, in most cases have suffered pain, financial stress and even partnership problems which come between loving and beloved people.

If we could video the problems caused and the anxiety faced by parents as their children, who should have been the product of sincere and everlasting love, cause stress, worry and sometimes division to those who have loved and nurtured them through joyous times and times of great stress and trials. If we are not aware of the trauma and sorrow we inflict upon those who have protected and nurtured us through the times we could not act for ourselves. How then can we ever imagine the anguish that we inflict on our merciful Heavenly Father and the Son who gave all that we may share eternal life.

To say my children have not caused my wife and I, terrible heart pain, would not only be untrue but also delusional. I cannot recall the number of times I disobeyed my parents, came home late from school, when older, arrived home hours after they expected me, and watched as their tears of thanksgiving were altered to fits of anger.

So it has been with most children, they may have been chastised but never to extent of causing the pain and suffering as they do when older and forget that although they know where they are, and that they are safe, parents do not.

There seems to be that present day feeling that it does not matter if they do not recognise the celebration of birthdays, and even other events that mean so much to the family as a whole. Where has the emotion of caring gone when our children do not respect those who have done so much for them?

Is this the order of today? Is this because our children have lost all form and recognition of etiquette? The present generation that has little or no respect for the rights of any one but themselves.

Who can we blame? I may not have been brought up in a Christian household, but I was taught to respect others, I was taught right from wrong, my parents did care and did share their lives with me, and I did learn a very basic and elementary form of the Christian religion. It was this seed sown that blossomed and brought me to my Saviour's loving, caring arms, and allowed me to stand in awe of God and not in fear.

His promises to me are true, and providing you will believe in Him and accept Jesus Christ as your Saviour, you too will not fear death but know that the promise of Jesus Christ about the place He has gone to Heaven to prepare for all those who believe in him.

This is a chapter that one would hope would bring intelligent people to, or at least considering following Jesus Christ. There will be others who want further proof that the Bible can and does substantiate itself. In Isaiah chapter 3 and verses 16 to 26, we read, *"The Lord says, 'The women of Zion are haughty, walking along with outstretched necks, flirting with their eyes, tripping along with mincing steps, with ornaments jingling on their ankles.*

"Therefore the Lord will bring sores on the heads of the women of Zion; the Lord will make their scalps bald. In that day the Lord will snatch away their finery; the bangles and headbands and crescent necklaces, the earrings, bracelets and veils, the headdresses and ankle chains and sashes, the perfume bottles and charms, the signet rings and nose rings, the fine robes and the capes and cloaks, the purses and the mirrors, and the linen garments and tiaras and shawls. Instead of fragrance there will

be stench; instead of sash, a rope; instead of well dressed hair, baldness; instead of fine clothing, sackcloth; instead of beauty, branding. Your men will fall by the sword, your warriors in battle."

Could have Isaiah in about the year 760 BC, foreseen the great holocaust of the 1939 world war? Could this be the reason for enemies of the Jewish Nation and the Christian Church deny that this stain on humanity ever existed? Isaiah's writing the Prophesy from the Lord, is almost word for word of what happened to the Jewish women during the Second World War.

Parallels exist as the terrible horrifying stories and photographs as shown in newspapers of the day and at the movie theatres in newsreels. Tattooed numbers on arms, were as the Lord promised, branding; baldness as heads were shaved; fine clothing giving way to sackcloth; and perfume to the stench of overcrowded living areas. Ropes replaced sashes, and bullets replaced the sword as the Prophesy for the men was played out.

If Isaiah's writing did foretell the holocaust, and I believe it did, we now must examine other Old Testament writings and see if some of them have yet to befall on the world's human race. All of a sudden the prophesies of Revelation take on a new meaning, and the truth must be acknowledged that such plagues also promised of God, will happen.

Puny man has no answer to the might of God through nature, floods, droughts, fires; earthquakes are becoming an every day experience as countries worldwide are ravaged. World wide catastrophes causing so much devastation and loss of life, this time Australia and our neighbours in New Zealand felt the power of God's wrath.

The devastating earthquakes in New Zealand, floods, cyclones in the eastern states of Australia, fierce storms and cyclones in Western Australia should and must be viewed of God's disenchantment with the behaviour and the present day worship of money and material things.

The Book of Jonah tells of God sending Jonah to Nineveh to warn the people to come to repentance. He did, and from the King to the least citizen they repented and God held back His wrath. Jonah, chapter 3 verses 7 to 10, *"Then he issues a proclamation in Nineveh: 'By the decree of the king and his nobles: ' Do not let any man of beast, herd or flock, taste anything; do not let them eat or drink. But let man and beast be covered with sackcloth. Let everyone call urgently on God. Let them give up their evil ways and their violence. Who knows? God may yet relent and with compassion turn from his fierce anger so that we will not perish.' When God saw what they did and how they turned from their evil ways, he had compassion and did not bring upon them the destruction he had threatened"*

Unfortunately we in Australia are not so fortunate for our leader has left no doubt that as an atheist she does not believe that there is a God, so there is little chance of her inspiring the people to repent and turn again to the only One that can stay His wrath. We can be thankful that Australia and New Zealand were not as over populated as some third world countries where the death toll would have been counted in thousands, we can thank a merciful God for that.

We will not but we should! How many denomination leaders called special days for prayers or even open their buildings for community or private prayers? There were great examples of civil brotherhood with monetary and physical assistance, but as John Wesley pointed out that even evil can do goods things.

Will the enormous destruction bill for the damage done place more stress on the budget of these two neighbour nations? How much of the financial stress will be placed on the ordinary people in the community, will taxes, rates and other costs as the greed of those in power of the big and powerful companies forget that a dollar earned is a one hundred cents that can only be spent once?

Therefore could God's wrath extend to another world wide depression? As an average person who has lived through very trying financial times, I know that those in power on high incomes have forgotten that all are not as fortunate. We are also very lax in not teaching our children the value of money, consider the amounts spent by the young on mobile telephones.

Governments seem to be able to make financial decisions without a study on how best can their plans be instigated. One esteemed politician had his bill passed granting financial bonuses for babies being born, having seen the outcome of young inexperienced girls having babies and the problems that these girls, in their very early years have to face, my observation is simple, these children are not born from love as God planned, but from lust and greed for money.

A great financial crisis is going to happen not only with individuals, or companies but nations. We have forgotten what it is to pay cash, the plastic card has taken over, and the main difference in our dealings is not seeing hard cash change hands. Five twenty-dollar notes are more real than spending a hundred dollars on a card.

Our personal financial management has been shot to pieces; the older generation endured a depression, a world war, where we learnt to live within our means. We were expected to finance a war, every street was to become a War Savings Street, where our investments were directed into the manufacture of weapons use to kill and maim. Even school children were encouraged to save, and received a certificate if they raised one pound for the war effort.

Our present day children are not taught how to live in recessions or more serious world depressions. What they have in their pockets, in their banks are secondary to what is left on their credit cards. They run up accounts on mobile telephones which in the end, seriously damage their parent's financial security. We are already talking about teaching past history, but with no mind of teaching how our children should be prepared for the financial struggles that lay ahead.

The political powers are at a loss to reach agreement on climate change, smaller Pacific Ocean nations stand in real threat of tsunamis, ice caps melting, raising the level of the ocean and putting these low lying countries in jeopardy.

But the major powers will argue, when all they are interested in is self-preservation and their own financial security. It is sufficient to look at the present trials the world is enduring by the forces of nature, but we must acknowledge, these events, as foretold in the Bible are controlled by God.

What is more dangerous to our future existence is financial and caused by greed in wanting every thing without consideration of the future financial commitment. It is well to cost our assets against our liabilities but if and when the world's monetary system fails, our assets will have lost all or most of their value but our debts will remain the same.

Why is it not possible for a rich person to purchase the passport enabling them to enter the kingdom of God in heaven? Firstly credit or debit cards are not accepted, without a pen and cheque book one cannot write a cheque no matter what the bank balance states. As we are told we leave the world as we came into it, no purse, no wallet, no money. What is needed to enter the promised paradise?

You must believe in a merciful God, His sacrificed Son, and the Holy Spirit that guides us. You are an unworthy sinner, and stand before judgement as your earthly life is weighed up; it is then on the judgement of Jesus Christ, who will allow you to enter those glorious portals of the promised Heaven. Millions of currency will not insure you an entrance, but how you made that fortune and how wisely you spent it, will.

If after you had all you wanted, you considered the unfortunates of the world who are denied even their needs. Why should you live and eat of all the great provisions given by God and have no consideration for the hundreds of thousands scrapping up a meal by scavenging on the rubbish tips in countries that in some cases, many have more than enough to sustain themselves.

What will be the outcome of the problems besetting the Middle East? Only the future will reveal the future, for who can say the new regime will be more humane that the one deposed? Who can say that those who take on power will remember those who fought and died to win their freedom and that greed and lust for power may be the driving force in the new government.

We who have studied the Book of Revelation know that Jerusalem will surrounded by their enemies, so how do we know that the new powers will not be more active in achieving the fall and destruction of God's Holy Land?

What this proves, in my mind at least, is that in many of the prophesies, which some scholars claim to have happened, are yet to come. Also there is no rhythm in God's timing, it is at His choosing and at His direction when these prophesies are fulfilled. Being all merciful, if there is a glimmer of hope of revival to the true Christian Faith, and that man will acknowledge Him as the only true living God and recognise His Son

Jesus Christ as the Saviour, the end will not yet be.

God's time may appear to be much different to ours and a thousand years in our time may be just an instant in His. But it is not the year, but the state of man's standing with the Almighty that will determine that fateful Day of Judgement. This does not mean that we can estimate or know the times and seasons of God's will, for as time belongs to Him, He will make the decision of when that blessed second coming of His Son Jesus Christ will eventuate. Is your home adequate or luxurious? Is it furnished for your comfort or to gain the esteem of friends?

Is your motor vehicle sufficient for your needs or does it just add to your presumed prestige? All these are matters that you must address before you enter into the judgement we will all have to face in the after earthly life. There is no reason that a Christian can be comfortable, and God honours His promise of supplying your needs, but beware that effective tool of Satan, greed.

How do you believe Jesus will judge you? You had better assess your chances and make the necessary changes before you are called to answer. A lifetime on earth is but an instant, but why how you spend eternity is not a part of your planning? Will you plan for the little things and ignore the greater picture? In my youth as a lay-preacher, I travelled throughout Victoria, in those days on visits to country areas, four or five services were the normal rather than unusual. In the heat of the day one was required to preach in a suit, collar and tie.

When one showed compassion they would invite male members of the congregation to remove their coats to be more comfortable, in return one would hope the same courtesy would be offered to the preacher, not often was this offer given. These were the days when Clergy were distinguishable by their dress, the reverse collar was a give away.

Christianity it is where the dress is casual light and, I add comfortable, but was Jesus comfortable on the cross when He gave all for us? The robes that adorn a priest of many religious persuasions certainly show that they are different, so the question arises have we taken our casual approach to our worship of God too far?

Should the dress of an ordained Minister witness to his calling and station in the Church of Almighty God? A cross or a fish on the casual shirt may be a small witness but at least it is something. When we consider that those active in our community are recognisable by their dress, a policeman or woman is distinguishable by the uniform they wear and therefore can be identified when needed. The fire and accident workers also are easily identified, a doctor can be seen to have a stethoscope around his neck, so are ambulance, pilots, members of our armed services, we all know at a glance who they are and identify their area of expertise. So we have covered physical problems by the distinctiveness their dress, and know who to approach with our problem, but what about our spiritual aid?

The personal trauma of a motor vehicle accident, flooding, fire, or earthquake can in many cases have more serious repercussions than those physical ones. This trauma does not only effect those involved in the happening, but innocent by-standers can be affected and suffer. Immediate counselling by a trained person can alleviate some of the initial shock. In most cases a member of the clergy will be most helpful, but if we cannot recognise what they represent, why would we seek their assistance.

In my youth we as young Christians wore buttons with **JESUS SAVES** boldly printed upon them, this was our witness to God the Father of all mankind. The question must be asked and answered, are we ashamed of who we follow? What a better way to witness but to boldly show who we are than by the way we live and identifying ourselves with our Saviour.

May I borrow the words of Charles Hadron Surgeon, who over 150 years ago, said, **"the Christian Church is asleep. A loud voice is needed to awaken it."** A thunderous voice is now needed to awaken Christians world wide, to the fact that despite the number of denominations the true Christian Church is the Bride of Christ and is made up of dedicated followers of Jesus ordained by God, not man.

Such a person is already being fitted with great wisdom and understanding of what God's plan is, it would be very easy to place the qualifications needed for this chosen one to complete God's message to the whole world.

God is the only one who can fit them with all the talents needed to stop the world's decline into total moral oblivion. Who will it be? Only God knows, but we must pray that they will come and spark the greatest worldwide revival in the history of the world. There have been many who spoken up and lead thousands into the love of Christ. They were not giants in their field but were made great by the leading of the Holy Spirit.

We must not look for the greatest scholar in the Christian Church, but for simple person made great by by God Himself. Big and expensive Churches will not bring people to God, they may bring them to Church, but not to God. The simple truth is that like Jesus we have to go out into the streets, the fields, the stadiums where the people are. We must concentrate not on giving comfort to those who worship, but to those who do not know or have ever heard the name of Christ Jesus, his sacrifice on the cross and why he died for the sins of the world.

Firstly everyone must be acquainted of what sin is and that God's sentence for these sin's is death, not only earthly death but eternal death and damnation.

In closing this chapter, I sincerely pray that you may heed the warnings, look to God and pray for the future for a peaceful united Christian world. We as Christians must remember the many gods that were destroyed in establishing the Jewish nation, the world domination by the god - money will be destroyed and instead of worshipping financial riches, and we will return to worship a true and Living God.

www.ingramcontent.com/pod-product-compliance
Lightning Source LLC
LaVergne TN
LVHW041551060526
838200LV00037B/1241